My name is Vernon. I am Ojibwe.

Vernon indizhinikaaz. Indoojibwew.

I like walking about on the shore of the lake,

I Will Remember
Inga-minjimendam

I Will Remember
Inga-minjimendam

Kimberley K Nelson

Illustrations by Clem May
Gaa-anishinaabewisidood Earl Nyholm

Loonfeather Press
Bemidji, Minnesota

For my two girls, Kate and Amelia, my husband,
Elmer, and my friends in Red Lake and Ponemah.

KKN

Loonfeather Press wishes to thank the following for their support and encouragement: The George W. Neilson Foundation, Region 2 Arts Council through funding from the Minnesota State Legislature, and the Native American Arts Initiative through the McKnight Foundation. We are grateful.

Loonfeather Press
P.O. Box 1212
Bemidji, MN 56601

Niminwendaan babaamaazhagaameyaan jiigibiig,

and looking at all the little animals that are there.

imaa dash niminwendaan
ganawaabamagwaa anooj awesiinsag
imaa babaa-ayaawaad.

I like to go to school
and play with my friends.

Igo gaye niminwendaan
imaa dash apane ko
gikinoo ' amaagooyaan,
imaa dash apane ko
niwiiji ' aag niwiiji ' aagaansag.

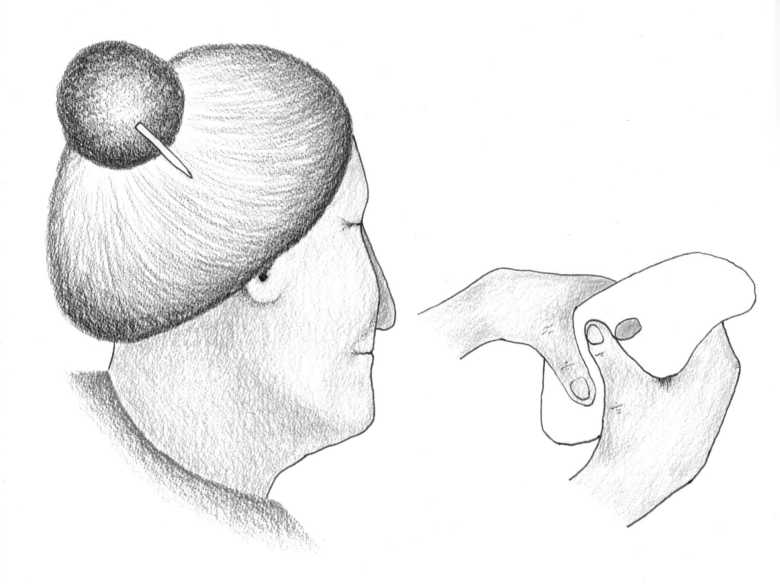

Where we live, I like watching my grandmother make fry bread.

Mii dash imaa endaayaang nimenwendaan ganawaabamag nookomis zaasakokwaaniked.

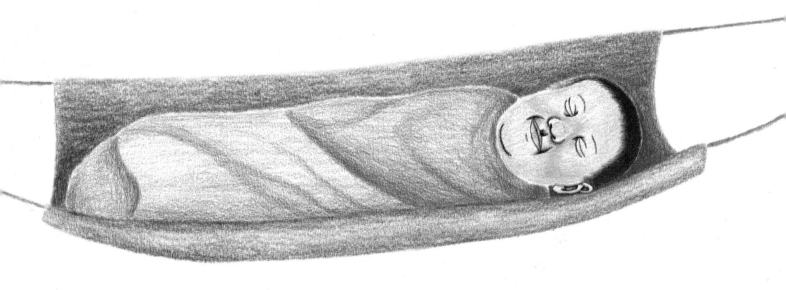

I like to watch the baby go to sleep.

Niminwendaan apane ganawaabamag nishiime
baabiinsiwid noonde-nibaad.

I like helping my father fish with nets,

Niminwendaan wiidookawag imbaabaa
bagida ' waad,

and my mother mends the nets near the shore.

a ' aw dash wiin nimaamaa imaa jiigibiig
dazhi-waapidasabii.

I really like to go to a pow-wow.

Aapiji niminwendaan
ji-izhaayaan imaa
endazhi-niimi ' idiwaad.

At the pow-wow I like to watch fancy dancing.

Iwidi dash niimi ' idiing niminwendaan
ji-mino-waabamagwaa naamijig
maamakaadeshimowaad.

And, I like to dance too.

Gaye niin niminwendaan ji-niimiyaan.

I like to swim in the lake in the summer,

Mii dash azhigwa ani-niibing niminwendaan
ji-bagizoyaan iwidi zaaga ' iganiing,

to hunt with my father in the time of autumn,

baamaa dash ani-dagwaagig niwii-wiijiiwaa
imbaabaa wii-pabaa-nandawenjigeyaang,

and when the lake is frozen over,
we will ice fish.

apii dash gashkading
i ' iw zaaga ' igan,
niwii-akwa ' waamin.

I like to listen to the grown-ups talk.

Niminwendaan apane ko bapizindawagwaa
gichi-aya ' aag gaganoonidiwaad.

But most of all, I like to listen to my
Grandfather tell stories. He tells all
sorts of legends to me, and about all
those things that he did when
he was small.

Memindage dash nawaj niminwendaan
ji-bapizindawag nimishoomis aadizooked. Mii
sa anooj dino gegoo aadizookawid, apane ko
ayinaajimotawid i ' iw isa gaa-izhichigegwen
gii-agaashiinyd.

And when he finishes, he says,
"Remember these stories, my boy,
because one day you will tell them
to your grandchildren."

Dasing eshkwaataad indig, "Noozis, Mii go
izhi-minjimendan onow dibaajimowinan,
baamaa dash igo ingoding gaye giin
giga-ani-dadibaajimotawaag ingiw
goozhishenyimag."

I, too, will remember these for the future.

Booch igo niigaan akeyaa inga-minjimendaanan
gaye niin.

Kim Nelson lives in rural Kennedy, Minnesota, with her two daughters, Amelia and Kate and her husband, Elmer. She worked at the Red Lake Head Start and school for ten years. In addition to writing children's books, Kim is a published artist and papermaker. She does artist residencies in area schools and speech/language pathology in the Kittson Central Schools. The family raises a large garden which provides plenty of plant fibers and flowers for Kim's papermaking and art.

Clem May is a young artist whose work reflects the activities and landscape of the Red Lake area in northern Minnesota where he lives. He has exhibited in several of the Ojibwe Expos, painted the mural for the new Red Lake High School, and does commercial fishing. **I Will Remember** is his first book illustration.

Earl Nyholm is professor of Ojibwe at Bemidji State University. He is co-editor of **Ojibwewi-ikidowinan, An Ojibwe Word Resource Book** and is a frequent presenter at workshops and other activities sponsored by the Smithsonian.